VIRTUAL SANDBOX
by Martynas Čeledinas

COPYRIGHT

VIRTUAL SANDBOX:

Copyright © 2021 Martynas Čeledinas

"You change your life by changing your heart."

Max Lucado

Since I could remember, I always wanted to be someone special. I wanted to change the world for the better. Nothing mattered to me more than to help others. I don't know how I became like that, but I tried to be a good person. I didn't become a doctor like my parents wanted and I didn't become a priest as my grandmother wanted. But somehow, every headline in the news knows my name. My name is John. Just John Mathews, the biggest name on all the billboards in the entire world.

Let's start at the beginning. It all began when Elon started the Neurolink project and he succeeded, but it didn't turn out the way he planned. He created a virtual world called Virtual Sandbox and everyone wanted in. At first, he tried to implant microchips into the brain. Some operations were successful, but some surgeries didn't go as planned. With the dangers of brain surgeries being too severe, he found another solution. It was called brain gel.

The brain gel was a substance that the head was immersed in with no surgical intervention. The gel captured the brain's electromagnetic signals and those signals could be transmitted electronically to a computer and from a computer to the main server. That server was named Virtual Box. Everyone wanted in and people immersed into the virtual reality, wanting to escape the real world and live in a stress-free life of luxury.

Sadly, this wasn't enough for some and soon many people stayed there permanently. Then Elon's company created artificial cocoons for their super rich clients. It turned out that as many as 15 percent of the world's population could afford this service and the virtual world kicked into high gear. Many wealthy people wanted to forget the problems of the real world and explore the luxury life of the Virtual Sandbox.

People inside the cocoons, fully immersed in a virtual reality, almost forgot about the real world completely. Everyone else just serviced the luxury life of those living inside the virtual reality one. The Sandbox economy was driving the real economy because they created all the wealth in the virtual world within it. Everyone who had capital was living inside the illusion of the virtual world. The citizens of Virtual Sandbox had new clothes, new cars, new houses, and even spaceships that denied the laws of physics, all at their fingertips.

They created new toys for the extremely rich, while the remaining 85 percent of the people, living in the real world, tried to make ends meet by working to sustain the world of Elon and buying a few days of luxury living in the virtual world whenever they could. Everyone knew they couldn't afford it but it was the biggest and most expensive ride in the world and they wanted a turn on it, no matter how short that turn was.

Hackers occasionally used their skills to access the Virtual Box but were quickly discovered by the cyber police and often paid a high penalty for the intrusion. But I had a secret way in because I was a cocoon pod engineer at one of the company's most heavily guarded facilities. My job was to handle the maintenance of the pods and I had a few days of maintenance access every week so that I could fulfil my role.

I was glad that I could secretly enter the world of the Virtual Sandbox. Nobody could blame the rich because the virtual life was amazing. Everyone looked like a model or a movie star. People were fit and good looking and they seemed happy. Everyone in the Sandbox left their problems back in the real world. People got in and out of relationships without a lot of thought but nobody knew who they were dating. It could be a man pretending to be a woman or a woman pretending to be a man. The fast pace of life was so rapidly changing that sometimes people moved apartment several times a week. Yachts and private planes were cheap, so people partied from dusk till dawn. But everything was fake. You didn't know who was who, or who was pretending and who was real. Most of the Virtual world looked like Monaco: clean, tidy, sweet and almost ideal. It was the idealistic paradise for the rich and privileged. Virtual companies were created in an instant and bankrupted in another. Virtual Sandbox was the biggest market the world had ever created.

The biggest companies in the real world usually emerged from the virtual reality. The newest cars, the most modern homes, the best new devices and even spaceship technologies were first drafted inside this world for the elite. The fast pace of life wouldn't be possible without this virtual economy. Everyone who was anyone was living inside a dream world and 85 percent of the rest were left to get on with it. Sometimes I would walk past those celebrities and they wouldn't even notice me. They thought I was just some nobody. I walked past streets so clean and polished like glass, but they were all fake and generated by the AI created by the employees of Elon. Those streets felt fake with fake people all around. They used fake avatar models created especially for them from their wishes.

Most of them weren't who they pretended to be. Some of them weren't really men and some of them weren't really women. The streets were full of fake smiles, fake cars, fake motorbikes and fake people. Nothing was real in this world. Some of the people had real businesses in the real world and managed their business from the Virtual Sandbox. Nothing was more important for those people than making big money to support their fake virtual life.

Although nothing seemed real in that world and was little more than bits of code sent from the server and received by human brains, there was one person. She was a singer. Her voice was amazing. She was a big celebrity in the Virtual Box and everyone went to the only place she would give a performance. That was the famous "Bridge" nightclub in Virtual Sandbox. She was the only person in the entire Sandbox who wanted to keep her own looks and didn't change her appearance. It was a bold move, and it paid off, because many people admired that she didn't want to alter her body type, look, hair color or anything else. She differed from the other people in the sandbox because she was natural and she loved how she felt.

The most important thing when you signed a contract with the Sandbox was that you could ask for one wish when you apply and the management was duty bound to fulfill it. Most wishes were simple, like wanting a car or a nice house. But some wishes are special, like hers for example. Her name was Simone, and she was with the Sandbox from the beginning. She had long dark hair, beautiful brown eyes, a slim body and looked young for her age. Her dad was one of the big corporate types and signed her in after her mother's death. Simone couldn't cope with the real world after her mother's loss, and the only way she could relax was in the Virtual Sandbox. I fell in love with her the first time I saw her. She was amazing, and she was the only authentic person in the whole virtual world, so I knew that one day I would be with her. I just didn't know it would happen so soon.

One year later.

I took her to my apartment. She was weak and restless. She seemed like someone who had been dreaming her entire life. But there was something about her that mesmerized me. I knew she had been living in that fake world for a long time and everything felt new to her. Her body was slim and elegant from the vitamins she received in the pod. The right number of calories for the right body type and the right number of nutrients for her digestive system sure kept her in prime condition. I knew she had the best doctors taking care of her but lack of movement and exercise had made her weak, and now she needed more rest than a normal person did.

Somehow she had forgotten how to live in the real life; she had forgotten the feeling of a touch and she had even forgotten how to walk.

She had been living in the virtual world since she was twenty-one. Now she was past her thirties but she still looked as beautiful as her avatar in the virtual box. I laid her on the couch so she could relax and sleep a little. The whole night I lay beside her and looked at her amazing beauty. She was short with dark hair and sparkling dark brown eyes. Her lips were full and a soft cherry color. Her smile could make any man fall for her. That night was the most wonderful ever, because the girl of my dreams was lying next to me all night.

When I woke up I felt relaxed and full of new hope. I was thrilled to be alive. It was the most beautiful day of my life. I wanted to tell everyone that I was the happiest man in the world. The problems in my life didn't matter anymore. I felt relaxed. I could dream again this night, and my new hopes and dreams made me feel alive.

She woke up pretty tired and wanted something to drink. I made her some green tea, and she drank the whole cup. She was mesmerizing. Somehow her smile filled the room. The Virtual box company tried to keep their customers in good shape, because the health of the body was equally important as the health of a mind in the virtual world. People received all their nutrients through an injection directly into the bloodstream. This way the company could manage the health of the clients thoroughly. The artificial cocoon was the most advanced piece of equipment in the world and all the patents were kept safe and taken care of in a top secret environment. People were the company's major commodity, and this strategy was promoted in all the commercials and all over the news.

Simone looked tired. I had dragged her across the entire city in my old and run-down Tesla, but somehow I had succeeded in saving her. I knew that kidnapping laws were strict and I could even face the death penalty for my actions, but still I was determined to save her life. I knew she had only me to count on, because other people wouldn't believe the things that I knew.

Her brain was degenerating, and she needed to use it as much as possible. The biggest flaw with the Virtual box wasn't in technology; it wasn't even with health systems in the cocoons. The biggest flaw was the human brains themselves. You see, our brains solve logical problems, like complex mathematical equations and creative problems like how to write a song or do the simple things like where to put our feet when we walk. Our brains need constant work on something and if it doesn't get its exercise, we just become a vegetable. Simone had a key problem with her brain. She had been in sleep mode for years in the Virtual box. Her neuroplasticity abilities had practically degenerated to zero. She was more like a baby than a young woman. I needed her to learn the basics again because I knew that if she didn't, she would end up having long-term medical issues.

She looked up and smiled at me. She wanted to stand, but somehow she fell to the ground.

"Are you hurt?" I asked.

"No I'm fine," she replied, but her words belied the truth.

"But you fell on the ground," I said.

She sighed. "I just have to get used to this world I guess."

I reached out my hand to her. "Let me help you up."

I took her in my arms and helped her stand. She was exhausted, so I carried her to the sofa. Simone actually hadn't forgotten how to walk; she had just forgotten how to use her brain again. My lovely singer tried to get up once more, but after few seconds she fell again.

"Relax," I insisted. "Get used to your brain again, it needs time. Give it time."

Simone stated, "I feel so clumsy. You probably don't like me anymore."

She smiled weakly.

"No," I smiled. "I like you just the way you are. You just have to learn how to use your mind and let the neuroplasticity kick in again. I know a good neurosurgeon. He's my friend and he could help us."

"I'm giving you so much trouble," she sighed. "It would have been better if you'd left me in the virtual world."

"No, don't talk like that. We have to try everything we can."

She smiled again and was almost resigned to my help. "Ok when we could see him?"

"I will call him right now," I said.

"Okay," she said softly. "Let's try that."

I called my good friend. He was a renowned neurosurgeon and brain specialist but most of all he was someone I knew I could trust. After a few minutes of talking he told me to come to him as soon as possible.

I carried Simone to my Tesla and we took the long road to another city. The journey was wonderful; I turned on my 80's music collection and we just enjoyed the ride. We joked and smiled along the way and she seemed to be feeling better and better as the time passed. Somehow her face seemed more alive and energetic the more we chatted. The first time I saw her she had looked really pale, but now she looked like a human being again.

We drove to a gas station, and I stopped and bought her some ice cream.

Simone licked the ice cream and her face lit up. "Wow, that tastes so good."

"It's just real," I said.

"I mean I can really taste the flavor," she replied. "It's the real deal. Every ice cream I had before seems tasteless compared to this one."

"Wait till you taste Coca Cola, Pizza and Tacos," I laughed.

Her eyes went as wide as saucers. "You have Coca Cola here?"

"Yes, we do. They developed it in the real world."

"I thought that Elon invented it."

I laughed again. "Nope, he didn't."

Simone considered the information for a few seconds as she thoughtfully ate some more of the ice cream. "Hmm, your world differs totally from Virtual box."

I could see that it was going to take quite a lot to get Simone to become used to life in the real world and probably more than just a taste of real ice cream.

"Yes, it does," I admitted.

Suddenly Simone's attention as drawn to something on the other side of the street.

"Who is that man with a sign on the street over there?" she asked.

"He's homeless," I said.

"What does that mean?" she asked innocently.

"It means he has nowhere to live."

"I don't understand," she said. "Why doesn't he just get a loan?"

"A bank probably won't give him credit," I replied.

"The bank in the virtual world always gives credit," Simone stated confidently. "Money is endless in Sandbox."

"This isn't your world Simone," I said. "It's more complex here."

She sat for a few more moments, her gaze transfixed on the shabby man with nowhere to live and little hope.

"I don't understand why people have to be poor here."

"You have a lot to learn in this world," I stated and headed back to the car.

All through the journey I explained everything to her in the smallest of detail. She couldn't believe such things as war, politics, drugs, criminals and slavery existed in some parts of the world. Simone was like a child who didn't know anything of the real world. She was immensely curious and explaining things to her wasn't hard, but still many of the things that happen in our world terrified her. The shining world of Virtual Box clouded her mind from the actual problems of the real world and she was amazed and scared in equal measure when she understood how dangerous and fragile the real world could be.

"Why do people do such horrible things in your world?" she asked, once she had absorbed what I had told her.

"I don't know, really," I replied honestly. I really didn't know.

"Why do people go to war?"

"I don't know that either Simone. Things are like this in our world. It's our reality and we just live with it."

"Virtual box is so much safer than your world," she declared.

"Yes, you are right," I said. How could I have possible disagreed?

And then suddenly we fell into silence. Neither of us wanted to say anything more. It was as if the weight of the world's problems were upon us both and we had to bear them alone. Simone just looked through the window at the passing fields as I kept my eyes on the road as we headed for our destination. Suddenly, Simone sat upright as if she had become aware of an impending disaster.

"Something is wrong. I feel bad."

It took me by surprise and unnerved me a little but I tried to reassure her and said "don't worry, we are almost there. Just relax a little."

But Simone was anything but relaxed. She suddenly puked on the floor and now she looked scared. Something was definitely wrong with her inside.

I put my foot to the floor. We were close and it only took me another five minutes to drive to my trusted friend Luke's place. When we arrived, I dragged Simone out of my car quite unceremoniously and took her inside his private clinic.

"Luke, help me," I pleaded as he came to the door.

He took one side of Simone's limp body and we managed to get her into his treatment room.

"What happened to her?" Luke asked.

"It's a long story," I said. "Can you look at her?"

He pointed at a table. "Lay her on that."

There was lots of medical equipment and other medical gadgets lying around in his practice room. The technology he had wasn't new, but in his hands it did the job perfectly well.

After Luke performed a few tests he visibly relaxed and sat down in a chair.

"I don't understand. She seems fine, but there is definitely something wrong with her," he said. "I'll try to perform a brainwave test; I should be able to tell you more then."

"Oh my God, I haven't seen anything like this," James said. "Where did you find her?"

I shifted uncomfortably. "I took her from Virtual box."

"Are you crazy?" Luke exploded.

"I had no other choice. She was feeling bad and nobody else wanted to help her."

Luke seemed to understand that. "Okay, I see. The problem is that her brainwaves are distorted. It happens when someone isn't using their brain for long periods of time. The brain functions similar to a muscle. It needs to handle real-world problems. If it doesn't it simply deteriorates. This is how neuroplasticity works. The brain has to have challenges all the time to function properly. Her problem is that she was in a sleep mode all the time and her brain forgot how to work."

"Can you fix her?" I asked.

"I don't know, but it's good that you got her out when you did. A few more months and the process would be irreversible."

"What's your advice?" I was desperate for anything that could help Simone.

"She needs to live in the real world," said Luke. "Because it's a certainty that the virtual one will kill her."

"But after some time people will know she is missing," I said. "I wanted to get her back soon as possible."

"If you take her back now she will die." Luke's statement was matter-of-fact and almost unfeeling. "She has to live in the real world, at least for a year."

"For a year? Are you kidding? The police will sentence me to life in prison for this."

"There is no other choice," Luke replied. "But there is a bigger problem. Possibly there are more people like her and if the general population find out there would be an economic downturn for the Virtual box investors. Such information is very dangerous for them and they will do everything they can to hide such leaked info."

I knew what he said was true but it didn't make it any easier to swallow.

"You mean now I am a criminal and I'm going to be chased after by some corporate dudes who think I know too much?"

"Yes," said Luke.

"Are you kidding me?"

"No I'm not. You're in big trouble I don't know how you will get out of this. But believe me a life in prison is one of the pleasant choices, because corporate doesn't tread lightly on its sensitive information, especially a multitrillion-dollar business like Virtual Sandbox."

"We can call Elon. He could help." It was a desperate idea. How on Earth would I find Elon's phone number? And even if I could his security would never allow the call to go through to him. Luke seemed to read my thoughts.

"Are you kidding me? Elon is on Mars. How can he help you? The new CEO of Sandbox is a real pain in the ass. He denies all the claims of problems with neuroplasticity and because of the changing corporate high gains he will never allow this information to be leaked out. You not only put Simone in danger. I am also involved; now they could want my head too. The corporate environment these days is tough and someone who would want to oppose Max Styles is an idiot. He got through the corporate ranks like a tiger, wiping out everyone in his path. He's the world's second richest man after Elon and he will never give up his status. I know people like him, he's dangerous like hell and murder isn't a problem for this man."

"Then what should we do?" I asked. I was totally lost.

"I don't know John," said Luke after a while. "I really don't know."

A year before.

I got some sneak peeks into the world of Sandbox from time to time, from the old life pods destined for refurbishing. I can tell you only one thing; that life in the sandbox was something beyond my wildest imagination. People were open to everything; new ideas were being given out like free ice-cream. Everyone wanted to get into the big leagues inside the virtual world. Big league meant big money, enormous investments and giant gains. Nothing interested the small fish more than to have a great contract in the Virtual Sandbox where all the sharks were playing their financial games. Everybody knew that every NHL and NBA player had their connections, every business and every major financial player, every bank and financial institution, every country and everyone who really mattered had their presence in the box. Everybody could see if you were nobody because you would dress cheap, wear cheap digital cologne, and had a cheap haircut or a cheap beard. Status mattered above all else in this place.

The thing everybody wanted was the big ticket for the priciest ride in the whole Sandbox, where all the sharks threw away money like crazy in their New Year festival. Every year they held it in the marvelous cruise spaceship Trinity. This was the one place where dreams became a reality, where trillions were spent, where all the new deals were made. Most people in the world could only dream about the ride through endless space in Trinity when the clock turned midnight. The ball was where princes would meet their princesses and Cinderella stories became reality, and the place where enormous investments met new ideas and sealed the fate of billions for the year to come. I knew that, and everyone who had any brains also knew that Trinity was one of the most dangerous places to be. A wrong word or a wrong handshake could mean the end of your career or even the end of your life. Many people wanted to avoid that place, but the brave girls wanted to meet the man of their dreams inside that cruise spaceship and kiss them when the clock struck twelve. It was the dream of every girl in the world and all the men in the world knew that.

Somehow all my blessings came into my life when I was least expecting them. The economy was in turmoil, all of my friends were chasing after their own dreams and all I was left with was my boring job of Sandbox technician and engineer. All of my friends had already started their families, got themselves well paid jobs at big companies or their own businesses. It left me with my virtual reality pods that didn't give me the satisfaction or the finances I wanted. But still I had a job, and that mattered in that economy. Many people just got their universal basic income, and that was it. It was enough to subsist on and you could get by, but no girl in the world wanted to have a family with the person who played PlayStation 12 all day long and ate Doritos on the couch, while living in his parent's basement. Sorry guys, but if you are one of those you should think about your life choices and do something a bit more productive and exciting. It only gets harder when you get older, believe me.

At least I had a job. It was a boring one, but it was still a job and when I go to the bar to pick someone up, at least I got to talk about something. Believe me, it makes me stand out in the crowd who just want to get some attention from the females. And I still have my gang. Yeah, my gang, the ones I can call my genuine friends. Mark was a programmer in one of the major firms. He's smart as hell and works in AI programming for the Virtual box. We have many things in common. He hates me for the ability to use pods whenever I want, but that's life and I will never have his programming skills. Luke is a pretty good neurosurgeon and brain specialist, who works in his own private clinic. He got married not so long ago and lives with his wife at a beach resort. You can say he works for the rich and famous. With his skills he could go much further, but he doesn't like to talk about it. James is a great security specialist at the Sandbox. He knows everything about cables, wireless technology, routers and data transfer technology like 9G and 7BG. They specially developed BG standard for the Virtual Box, because of the large data transfer needed for the virtual world. It was developed by Elon's "Boring" company and used by the countries that have enough funds to support such technology. Only the major economic players could afford it and it meant everything for big businesses. Wall Street was throwing everything at the technology when it first came in. It was a big gamble, but it was sure worth it. The stock market skyrocketed after first IPO (Initial Public Offering) of the technology and the rest is history.

Me and my friends gathered almost every week to talk about new technological breakthroughs and where the Virtual box was headed. Engineers had so many ideas about the world that it was crazy. Sometimes even the military wanted to conduct their tests in the virtual world, but they forbid it in the virtual world act of 2032, when the first Virtual Box 4.0 servers were deployed.

The virtual world also solved the problem of the Corona virus outbreak in 2020. The lack of social interaction made people depressed and lonely, so people like Elon, Jeff and Bill stepped in to solve the problem and they introduced us to the concept of the virtual world.

At first the fees were minimal and everyone could get in. It was easy, you only needed a PC, Xbox or PlayStation and some virtual gear. But after a time, people didn't want to get out of the Sandbox. It was addictive and rich people wanted to go all in. Therefore, the life pods were created, and the Sandbox really took off. The rich had all the money in the world, so the virtual world had to accommodate their wishes. After all, big money drove not only the world's economy, but the virtual world as well. The prices skyrocketed and many people found that they could only afford a few hours of an ideal world that made everyone's dreams come true. Suddenly you could date superstars, you could fly a spaceship, you could battle enemies or do any amazing thing you liked. Virtual box was as big as our solar system and there were rumors that it was actually bigger, because there were leaks of information that the elite were flying on spaceships through the entire Milky Way, but anyone who knew more would mysteriously and suddenly disappear and the rumors could never be confirmed.

I always wondered if there could be a world hidden behind the asteroid fields of our solar system, tucked away in the virtual world. That possibility bothered me and all of my friends. They thought the Sandbox was far bigger than we knew and that dangers were everywhere. Some of us thought that the virtual world spanned several galaxies and even featured alien life. But that was all a big secret hidden behind the closed doors of an enormous company. The founder of Virtual box, Elon, was somewhere on Mars, busy making a second planet habitable for human life. He had his hands full and he didn't have time to explain to the public about the secrets of the virtual world he had created. We ourselves were too far removed from the heads of the corporate elite to get to this kind of secret information, and who would listen to people like us anyway? We had no stakes in the company; we possessed no stocks, and we were just second guessing. But eventually time would show that we had been right.

Every Friday, me and my friends gathered at our favorite local bar to discuss politics and new ideas. The news was almost always the depressing same blend of poverty in Africa, war in the Middle East and of course new technologies in the Virtual box. Every day people thought of something new to bring to this virtual world, and it was improving at an exponential rate. New cars, new bikes, mystical animals, luxurious apartments, giant yachts and incredible spaceships. Everything was new in Sandbox and because of the flexibility of the virtual world it was impossible to know what new ideas would be implemented next. Developers and designers could make almost anything they wanted, except the things that were beyond the laws of physics. After all, the virtual reality had to be a realistic one, so the common laws of gravity, energy and others had to be followed and it all had to be consistent.

The virtual world had everything that anyone could ever dream of, but you had to be very rich to live in it. After all, this beauty had to be sustained, servers had to be maintained, salaries for millions or even billions of people had to be paid. All that beauty and luxury had to be financed somehow. Many things in the Virtual Box were so new and so paid up that many did not know it even existed. There were things like new flower combinations from the world's leading botanists, the best car designs from the world's leading automakers, the newest animal creatures from world-renowned biologists. It was crazy how many things were driving the virtual economy and how many people were involved. The majority of those in the Virtual box didn't even know how much effort was made to sustain the luxury life of the virtual world.

Everyone wanted to get in, but nobody wanted to get out. Perhaps the easiest way to get out of the virtual world was to hurt somebody, either physically or psychologically. Violence wasn't allowed in there and everybody knew that rule was one of a few fundamental ones that simply could not be broken. Many people couldn't understand why it was so important to obey these rules, but it was a standard that they all had to follow.

But something was missing in that world and that something was more obvious for the people who spent more of their time in the real world. It was a sense and taste of the real thing. People had all the wealth and influence they could handle, but they just cared for themselves, they just knew what they wanted and didn't consider the lives of others who were less fortunate. Some people in the virtual world left their sick mothers or fathers, they left their grandparents in nursing homes. They wanted what was best only for themselves, without considering the lives of others. They were thinking only about their wants and desires. Eventually their pasts would catch up with them and their virtual businesses would crumble like any other business in the real world that was not properly cared for. Because the truth always gets out, no matter how much you try to hide it. We always want to achieve something bigger than ourselves and that's our strength, but we still have to care for the ones who are weaker than us as well, because if we don't society will fall and we will fall with it. We have these amazing achievements; we have all these skills, but we value them only from our perspective, while we forget the lives and hardships experienced by many others.

I gathered with my friends one day at the bar. We were all in good spirits and ordered a few beers. After about an hour of conversation,

James mumbled something about Virtual Box having a security flaw and this one, if misused, could get many people in trouble.

"But you run the security, can't you fix it?" I asked.

"It isn't that simple," James replied. "This security flaw lies in the kernel code of the system and nobody wants to mess with that. I addressed the problem many times, but the management told me to forget about it."

"So we are using an insecure system?" I pressed.

"Yes. But nobody should know about it."

"You know nothing gets out from us," said Luke.

He was speaking the truth. There was no way any of us would have blabbed about anything, especially something as big as this.

"I know," James smiled. "That's why I told you."

"But how can they run this system like that?" I asked. It seemed crazy.

"I think they left it for a purpose," said James. "They engineered the flaw to be like this in the first place. It means they engineered it from the first kernel of the system. It looks like they have a reason for it."

"Some secret door for someone who had big stakes in the company?" I suggested.

"I wouldn't be surprised if Elon engineered it himself," James grunted.

"That's crazy," I replied. I couldn't believe that Elon would do something like that.

"Maybe. But someone could use this back door for evil purposes," James concluded.

James really believed that they left this hole on purpose and his blue eyes sparkled, because he was certain that he had found something and it was big. I had to agree with him. After all, he was a Sandbox security specialist who knew what he was talking about.

"Okay James," I said. "Let's say you are right. It, could be really dangerous for the system, but if the management doesn't want to get involved you probably should keep your distance from the matter."

"I think you should keep your mouth shut, James," Mark chipped in, "because if the word gets out you could be in big trouble. I know that recently a hacker used a loophole in the Virtual Box and they sent him to prison. Also, he got a huge fine for revealing the information."

Mark was right. All the hackers who used weaknesses in the virtual world had to endure harsh consequences if they were caught and if James was to reveal such a loophole to the public, he would suffer the harsh fate of a lone wolf who would be taken down quickly. James smiled at Mark and agreed with him. After all, nobody wanted to mess with the biggest company on the planet. We all knew that dealing with corporate power always leads to big problems for small fish like us.

The atmosphere in the room became subdued; we all knew that we weren't as strong as we thought. We all had to deal with the virtual world, but we wanted that our lives would matter. We were like small fish who wanted to be like the biggest sharks in the ocean. Nobody knew that after a year we would be known to everybody in the world and we would take our places in the history books.

"Guys cheer up," laughed James. "Why so sad? Let's raise our beers an shout to the world that we are the greatest."

"Yes, let's drink to Elon and his Neurolink technology that got us so far into the future," Mark yelled.

"To Elon and Virtual Box, to the stars and beyond," we chanted in unison. It was a carefully rehearsed line that we always used.

We all drank a lot of beer that day. Mark quickly found himself a girlfriend and disappeared into a dark spot near the bar. She was a young student who had her eyes on him that evening. She kissed him and her small fingers ran through his short hair. He smiled and his strong, muscular hands that were lifting weights three times a week were on her hips. She smiled back at him and her breath was taken away by his strong lips going over her neck. They were into each other for an hour and later that evening they both disappeared into the night. Probably the man of the hour took her to his apartment. Luke left early too as he had to take his wife to work early in the morning, so he said his goodbyes and departed, leaving only James and I to chat. We had a few more beers, talked about Virtual box for some time and after getting bored we headed for home. That day was good. Mark got what he wanted, Luke was home in time to meet his wife, James got his attention for finding a secret loophole in the virtual world and I got my beers.

Next day I secretly connected to the Virtual box, probably because those beers gave me the courage to do it. That day I wanted to see her. The virtual bar was full, but I found my spot. Her songs were as beautiful as they always were. Her music inspired me. She was the only one that I respected in the virtual world. She wasn't pretending, hiding, manipulating, or acting out. Simone was real. She was probably the only authentic person in the whole box. She inspired so many people and all the girls wanted to be like her; strong, independent, confident and ready to take on anything. She was the biggest star that everyone knew and I think I loved her. Her beautiful legs made her go through a stage like she was on water. Simone's sparkling brown eyes shone like diamonds in the sky. Her long, shiny hair ran across her shoulders like silk. Her smile and beauty made men breathless. Every time she was on stage, her energy captured those who listened to her. She had a warm, soft voice that echoed through the internet like a symphony. Her performance mesmerized me and I looked at her like a fool who wanted the attention from a woman that was way out of my league.

When I returned home, I slept like a baby. I had a strange dream where Simone would call for me; she seemed to be in pain and was drowning. I reached out with my hand and grabbed her; she smiled at me and I woke up. That was a strange dream and I wondered what it meant.

The next day I spent my time fixing a few broken life pods. Something was wrong with the pod health systems. There was an unknown problem that was strange to me, so it took a few days to finally fix them. The pods were old but reusable. The new pods, which had a very broad spectrum of health technologies, were rolling out from the factories and the company had lots of money, but I still had lots of work on the older ones. Many new technologies were strange to me and the older pods were better in many ways than the new ones. After all, the boring company initially designed them and the new ones were just a simple, cheap rip off of the originals.

Something was strange however, the data on the pods suggested that the brain activity for the people who used these particular models had decreased. That wasn't good, but I didn't make something out of it, because they were old pods and data could be inaccurate. I had worked like hell that day and my mind was full of information; I knew I had to rest and headed home. That night I slept and had a strange dream. I was with Simone; she kissed me and I kissed her back passionately, exploring every part of her lips and mouth. It was the best dream I had ever had, but it couldn't last and I eventually woke up.

The next day I was tired and I wanted to relax, but my work kept me up and going. My hands felt like lead weights and I wanted to get to bed, but I had 3 more hours to work. When I got home I felt drained, like a lemon. My hands felt weak, and I dropped onto my bed like an old run down horse. I had a good sleep and the next day I was fresh and running through my work again. I wanted to walk inside the virtual world, so I sneaked into one of the unused pods and immersed my mind into the Virtual box.

I was walking down the road looking at one of the beautiful cars that I had always wanted and bumped into her.

She smiled at me and introduced herself.

"Hi, my name is Simone."

I was stunned that she was speaking to me and stammered, "Hi, I know."

"You 're someone new," she said. "I've never seen you before."

"Virtual world is a big place," I mumbled.

Her hands went through her beautiful long hair and she replied.

"But I know almost everybody."

I was afraid that I would get caught illegally using the pod so I knew that I had to think fast.

"I'm new here, that's why you've not seen me around."

She smiled. "Hmm, so who are you? Are you a billionaire investor or a basketball star? Or maybe a movie star?"

"It's a secret," I teased.

Simone's eyes lit up. "Oh, I love secrets. Why don't you come with me?"

She took my hand, dragged me through the enormous crowd and gave me a tour of the immediate surroundings, pointing to a group of young men

"You see those guys with strange cars? She asked. "They are basketball superstars. I dated one of them. They are really boring. Those guys with the fancy clothes? I don't even want to remember them. They are some billionaire's children, really rude and bad mannered. Do you see that guy?"

"Yes."

"Never get involved with that one. He's Russian mafia, very dangerous."

"Okay I won't but..."

"See this guy?"

"Yes."

"He's a big movie producer, I would like to star in his movie one day, but don't tell anyone."

"Ok I won't."

Simone seemed to know who everyone was and her quickfire introductions to who they were was overwhelming as I struggled to keep up.

"Do you see that gang over there?" she asked.

"Yeah," I said. "They look cool."

She smiled and said, "Come on, let's talk to them."

We walked over to the group of young men who were hanging around chatting with one another. They spotted Simone almost immediately and I could tell that they obviously thought a lot of her.

"Simone, how are you?" asked one of the gang, a skinny guy who was wearing a huge and expensive watch.

"Hi guys," said Simone. "This one is new here" she continued, by way of introducing me to them.

"Hello," I said weakly. Somehow it didn't seem like it was enough.

"These guys are in a band," said Simone. "They are named "The Spaceship Virus." They're really cool."

" How are you all?" I asked.

A tall and muscular looking guy with thick black hair stepped forward. He seemed to be the leader of the gang and spoke with a certain authority.

"I'm Max," he said, holding out his hand. I shook it.

"We are busy preparing for a big day coming up," he said.

"What big day?" I asked innocently.

"You don't know?" laughed Max.

I shook my head.

"Are you from another planet or something?" Max asked and they all laughed at the joke.

"No, I'm from Earth," I replied, somewhat indignantly.

Everybody laughed again and I felt a little uncomfortable.

"We are performing at Trinity on the New Year," Max explained.

"But that's 9 months away," I said.

"It's Trinity," explained Simone. "They can't mess up. They have to prepare and synchronize the holograms, the space fireworks and everything else. There's a lot to get right."

Max nodded. "Big companies are investing in us. We have lots and lots of stuff to organize, write lots of contracts and prepare the music."

Max, with his giant avatar, looked at me and smiled.

"It seems you 're going big this year," I said. It was a massive understatement.

"They will be the biggest thing in the box until the clock strikes twelve on New Year. Everybody knows about them. They will be huge," said Simone.

"Hell yeah," said Max. "We are going to storm the box."

"Congratulations you guys, I said. "That's going to be a big step forward."

"It's everybody's dream," said Simone. "Everyone would like to step onto the stage of Trinity and sing to billions of people all over the world."

Suddenly, Max jumped forward. "Simone, I have an idea."

"What's that?" she asked. "Could you sing one song with us?"

"You really would like that?"

"Of course. Sure. Absolutely," the chorus from the gang came back.

"Okay," said Simone, "but only one song."

Simone smiled, and her face lit up like a Christmas tree.

"Tomorrow we have rehearsal at ten AM, don't be late," said Max.

"Okay, I won't," said Simone and took my hand to lead me further down the street.

She was still smiling and happy, like a child who got a first taste of ice cream. She pressed closer to me and her warm artificial body was next to mine. I knew this was just a simulation but feeling her body close to me still made me happy and whole. She was someone from a dream that inspired my wildest imagination.

"Do you want to eat?" she asked after a while.

"Yeah, sure. Why not?" I said.

"There's a good place in Chinatown. I like Chinese food," she grinned.

I smiled back. "Yeah, I like it too."

We got ourselves to the digital Chinatown and ordered some food. I couldn't believe the tastes they had there.

We had food with holograms that tasted like an angel put his wings on our tongues. The servers all looked like Chinese supermodels and the music was amazing; it was so beautiful and deep like I had never heard before. All the staff knew Simone and gave her the best of food and tastes. For other people, I looked like someone from another planet. Many people didn't know who I was and some thought that I was a new billionaire who invited Simone to a diner, so they were very sweet and generous to me. Simone was really sweet to everyone, and many people noticed that and complimented her. Somehow that bright person lit up the place with her kind heart. Nobody could resist her.

This Chinese place was the best restaurant I have been to in my entire life. Somehow the only thing that gave me chills in that place was the bright smile on Simone's face when she was talking with me. She seemed very interested in me; we had many things in common, and I told stories about my family and jokes that circled in the web. We talked about life and stuff that were important to us, like books, movies, the environment, music and Virtual Box. She was interested in my life and that made me like her even more.

When we left the restaurant we walked down the street and suddenly a warm rain fell from the sky. I took off my jacket and covered her head with it until our eyes met and we both smiled. I leaned my head slowly and our lips touched. It was so warm and beautiful, like I had never experienced before. She smiled at me again, and I felt like I was drowning in her eyes. Now I kissed her again, but this time it was more passionate and urgent. It was like a dream come true. I was kissing the most beautiful girl in the world. I knew that this was just in the virtual world, but I had never felt such happiness before.

Somehow, everything in my life now changed. Management gave me a raise. I avoided toxic people in my life and spent more time with my real friends Luke, Mark and James. They were happy that my life was changing, but I didn't tell them why. I wanted to keep my passion for Simone a secret, after all my connections to Virtual Box were illegal and I didn't want them to get in trouble. Our visits to the bar became more frequent. Every few months Mark got himself a new girlfriend at the bar, but women didn't mind his affections. After all, Mark was good looking and had a thing for the ladies and young girls also had a thing for him. Our days went on like that in a haze of beer, with more smiles and more laughs. We talked about many interesting things and told many funny stories to each other. Our friendship was solid as a rock and the real deal.

I visited Simone more and more. She probably knew I had low credits, so she helped to pay a few of my virtual bills from time to time. She was a great person, and I didn't mind her helping me out occasionally. Things were expensive in the virtual world and I couldn't always pay for some of the things I wanted. Simone had lots of money, so it was never a problem for her. She definitely didn't choose me for my bank account, and that was all that mattered to me. It was actual love at first sight and we both knew that.

We visited many awesome places, jumped from planes, attended luxury balls, drove supercars, sailed on super yachts, ate in the best restaurants, attended bike races and flew to the moon and Mars. We were into each other like nobody else; I knew every inch of her and loved her every centimeter, and she was into me in the same way.

Friends could see that I had changed somehow, but it didn't matter, they were my best friends and they were happy for me. In any case, they liked the new me and accepted the person I was.

A few months flew by like they were just days. After all, time flies when you are happy. Me and Simone where into each other and I tried to be with her as much as I could. I pretended to my managers that I was working overtime, but actually I was spending more and more time in the virtual world. One day my manager even gave me a bonus for my hard work. So everything was getting better and better for me. I wanted to buy a new car, but my old Tesla seemed to run fine for me, so I reconsidered.

Somehow life was getting sweet, the girl of my dreams took me to the best parties and the best shows in the Virtual world. I didn't want her to spend money on me, but somehow she knew my pockets were empty and didn't mind spending a few coins to help me get by. I felt bad for that and I wanted to compensate her somehow, but I didn't know how to do it just yet.

Also, I couldn't tell her about my illegal entry into the Virtual world, because I was afraid that she wouldn't like me anymore or treat me different. She was like a dream come true for a guy like me and I wouldn't leave her for anyone. Our kisses in the moonlight on the beach were wonderful. I felt like I was giving her all the best of me and that was all I could give her, because I was an illegal immigrant in this marvelous virtual world. We got ourselves a modern car that was fancy and cool. That ride represented our freedom from the world. The wind, when we were riding through the open roads of the virtual world, blew through her hair and made it look like a flowing dress. We were free and no one could reach us; we were like the dreamers of the future, attached to nothing and responsible to no one. That dream of freedom and hope kept us together and united us. Somehow we made a picnic and sat down on the grass of one mountain with a marvelous view of the sea. I looked into her eyes and smiled.

Everything was clear. Her mind was clear and her feelings for me were obvious. I was a nobody, but here I was having dinner with the most wonderful person in the Virtual Box. I didn't know what she was thinking but I was certain she had feelings for me. She was someone that inspired me, because of who she was and what she represented. Somehow, everything made sense. Everything that this person said and what she wanted was deep and moving. She knew about the problems in our real world, but she didn't know they were so deep and so hard.

Many people in the real world lived from paycheck to paycheck, sometimes struggling in poverty and despair. The virtual world was different, full of abundance and happiness, with no struggles or worries. Many people tried their best to reach that life of prosperity, but most failed. The virtual world was different. The abundance was endless and immeasurable, and the Virtual Box stocks were skyrocketing every single day. Somehow, everything in that world was different, because the money was pouring in from so many different donors.

I loved Simone, and I knew I would be with her no matter what, but I was hiding my secret and I didn't want her to know about it. I didn't want her to know that I was an illegal immigrant. Everything was wonderful; our days flew by like water flowing through the river. Everything in this world was precious. Every moment meant that we would be together. Our lives were full of joy and happiness. We were inseparable, like the two sides of a coin. We had lunch at the highest restaurant in town. The love of my life and I smiled at each other constantly that day and we had the most wonderful time of our lives.

We went to an ice cream shop. It was a small shop for people who wanted to taste the best ice cream ever created. It was so joyful and amazing. You could choose any type you wanted and it was so fresh it reminded me of the taste of fresh milk when my grandma milked a cow and gave me the first sip.

Somehow, everything was different in that world. They had the best tastes; they had the best rides; they had the best of everything, but everything felt different. Somehow, the small things mattered. I knew I loved Simone; I knew that for sure. But this world, the world without struggles, the world without ups and downs. Somehow it was different. Impossibly false. It seemed like a cover of a magazine, without any real pages in it and without the real problems. It looked real, but it obviously wasn't. All that glamour, glitter and shine didn't add up to anything. It was something, but it missed something too. It missed my grandmother, her soft smile and wonderful eyes. Her true love and care for others, her love for me, actual problems with cousins, and my parents, and for everything we held dear. No money in the world, no glamour, no glitter and no sparkles could ever have replaced that and no amount of virtual reality could create it either.

When I was little, the warm wind would blow through my hair and I was a free young child who was helping his parents and grandparents work in the open fields of a small country. We worked our asses off, but it was fun. We carried the hay through the vast fields near our small town to our barn and sometimes we used horses too. It was only a little town with poor folk who worked the land, but it had a lake near our house and we swam in it almost every day after our hard work in the fields.

The lake was wonderful. It had crystal clear, sparkling water and you could see your feet through it when you looked down as you treaded water. It was clean and wonderful and it had many different fish in it. Somehow, everything that was in that lake seemed magical.

There are so many wonders when you are young and it would be so good if you could stay that curious and open to life when you get older. Somehow everything in life has meaning; everything has its place in life. When you grow up you lose something important, in everyday work you lose the joy of life. That small sparkle that is really important. You go about your daily work; you clean your house; you mow your lawn, but life has to be more than that. It has to bring you joy; it has to be more open to many new things that come your way. Somehow everything that comes to your life should be meaningful. You can't just live like a robot every day and think that's okay. Have a purpose for something that makes your life shine. Have some little sparkle that fills your mind with happiness and joy. After all, we all are destined for greatness. Some people become truly happy just reaching their goals one by one, others find happiness in the eyes of their children, some people live for a righteous cause and some feel the presence of God in their work. Every life purpose is good as long as it helps other people and doesn't ruin the lives of others.

I looked back at Simone. She had a wonderful smile. I took her hand and we started dancing. She was surprised somehow. Probably nobody had ever asked her to dance on the empty streets of a virtual world where everybody looked at us like two crazy fools detached from reality. But that was exactly what we were.

Someone who could put a smile on the face of Simone was rare in this place. Somehow everyone was busy, and their schedules were full of meetings and new projects. The virtual world was filled with business owners, their lawyers, new project developers and new idea generators. Everyone was someone in this world; they represented their companies, brands, or business ventures. I was like a white crow in comparison. I was someone who was different in the pool of people who wanted to go big. I did not know about businesses, ventures or capital and I didn't have an agenda. I was just a small visitor in this big ride called the Virtual sandbox.

I liked the experience; somehow everyone who took part in it seemed intelligent and brave. The people I met in the Sandbox were sometimes more pleasant than the people in the real world. It seemed strange, but somehow I understood those people and why they wanted to escape. The business owner's world was tough. In the real world, you had to face the issues and the problems you encountered and you had to deal with them. But here in Virtual reality you immersed yourself in a world that was different. Most of the people here didn't have to deal with the problems that were common in the real world.

Sometimes I was sad for these people, they had so much wealth, but they were just the echoes of their past. Some of them had experienced trauma experiences that probably led them here. In reality, you had to face challenges of everyday life and do the hard work to reach your goals. That was a part of life after all. Go to work, and when you get home you have to make your dinner and you have to take care of yourself. Later in life, you maybe learn how to take care of others.

Life is hard, it's not simple, it takes effort, and it takes strength. Many people try to reach their goals and accumulate wealth to get into the Sandbox. But when you get there, then you are hooked. You reach a certain level of life and a certain lifestyle that immerses you in that fake world and you never want to get out of it. That idea made me scared a little. It has to make you scared, because after all, what happens if you can't get out of that Virtual World? If the surrounding lights are always so bright, then you might forget how the stars look in the night sky. Somehow everyone wants to get inside the Virtual Sandbox. But they might forget that they can get out of it.

The reality is hard, sometimes really hard, but after all, our brains are designed for reality, not for a sleep mode. I learned that in the first courses of cocoon pod engineering and I knew everything about human health, nutrition and even psychology. After all, at the initial stages of development it was suggested that these people in the pods would get out in the real world for some time and face some challenges, but somehow everything had changed after Elon went to Mars and new management of the Virtual Box kicked into full gear.

They wanted people to get addicted to the Virtual world and spend more time in it. Years went on and the people hooked to the system felt more and more distanced from the real world. After all, the technology was so new and so modern that everyone wanted to stay. People felt happy when they were distracted from reality, and that false happiness was addictive. You could become anyone: a business owner, an actor, a rock star, a car designer, a spaceship engineer. You could be anyone you wanted to be. That was the beauty of the virtual world. Many people in it wanted to be someone they were not, to escape the reality of their life. But Simone was the only exception. She was someone who really was the person she was. She wore no fake mask. She didn't have to hide anything; she was fully open all the time. Her mind was clear, like fresh water from a clean well. That amazed me, because I never met a person like her before, especially in a place like the Virtual Box.

I visited many wonderful places with her. We traveled to various countries, explored the pyramids, got to the Grand Canyon, and went to Tokyo to get some sushi; after all that we spent an amazing time relaxing at the beach and looking into the sunset. We kissed a lot and relaxed even more when we were together. We rode on bikes, into the sunset and dreamt about more adventures that we could experience.

Anything could happen, and the only thing that mattered was our love and happiness together. We were into one another and no one could separate us. We were like two sides of a coin, inspirable and bound to each other. Our love was undeniable. Her mind was full of me and my mind was full of her. Somehow the only thing that bothered me was her small drifts from time to time. I didn't mind it and many people in the Virtual Box had them. But I didn't have them and that bothered me somehow. Could I have been the only person who didn't have such small fades of mind in this Virtual world? The more I tried to not to think about it, the more it bothered me. Somehow I knew that this could be some unknown problem inside the Virtual Box, and some people like Simone could suffer serious consequences from it.

I looked at the times when Simone had those glitches in her consciousness and I knew right away that this was trouble. I disconnected from the cocoon pod and secretly looked at some information from the database. I knew that this could get me in serious trouble, but I still did it. The data seemed odd. Something was really wrong. I asked a manager if I could access Simone's pod, but he was strict and told me straight.

"That's high level access," he stated. "Only special personnel can get to that sector. Why do you need to access it?"

"Hmm sir. You know, hm; I have strange readings from this pod. The data seems strange and unusual," I stuttered.

"Show me," he said.

I brought it up on the screen.

"You see those teta waves?" I asked. "They are strange, you know, I think we should check them out."

He sighed. "You know, you're a good kid, John," he said. "But it's not our business to worry about stuff like that. It's not in our jurisdiction. There are specialists with higher pay grades than us who work in that sector. You know, if I were you, I would forget everything that you said and do your own work. You could get in trouble, son. You know some things like that could break your career. I know you lost your father a few years ago, but this thing, you know it has to stop. Do your work, you 're good at it, but keep away from things like that, okay?"

I realized that he was never going to back down. He couldn't. It was more than his job was worth. Maybe it was even more than his life was worth.

"Ok sir, I will," I said reluctantly.

"You are a good kid John," he smiled. "You will go far, I'm certain of that. Just keep away from trouble like this."

Now I really understood that something was wrong. My manager seemed scared when he understood that I knew something that I didn't need to know.

But for now I tried to stay away from Simone's pod, because I had stepped into some unknown territory and I needed things to settle down before I made any other move. After all, I had just uncovered something that was unusual and probably dangerous.

I wanted to spend more time with Simone and tried not to scare her about the information I had found. After all, she shouldn't have to bear my insecurities and my witch hunting.

We spent more time near the sea where we would watch the sunset and relax. We gradually came to know more and more about one another, our preferences, likes and dislikes, and our lives in general.

We went to a carnival where we had the most fun. Everyone was watching us, but we didn't care. We did the things we wanted and just as we pleased; we were ourselves and inspired everyone around us. Our minds were free, and like free spirits we were having the best time of our lives.

Simone's eyes were like the ocean; enormous and deep. She was so mesmerizing and was like nobody I had met before. Somehow she understood me and I understood her. Her warm hands and full lips where wonderful. I leaned my head to kiss her and slowly our lips touched. I was slow and gentle and she liked it. I looked into her eyes and smiled. Those days, completely in love with each other and filled with long and passionate kisses, were the best ever.

My mind went crazy from the passion and excitement when we were together. She was someone who was truly amazing and we always had the best time together. Somehow, everything was brighter and more in sync when she was with me. I would often run my fingers through her hair or across her body and I knew that she was becoming the most important person in my life. Her warm smile and sweet lips were the most wonderful things I have ever experienced and I wouldn't have given her up for the world.

Somehow, my problems faded through time. I was having the time of my life. People in the Virtual Box were generous to me and I tried to help them the way I knew best. I had lots of experience with tech and virtual word technologies so I was really valuable for those who knew less than me and I often helped them plan solutions for their technological issues.

Some people offered me money or contracts, but I knew I was an illegal immigrant to the Virtual box, so I gave away the information for free. It was dangerous for me to accept payment, because any large cash deposits in my account would look suspicious to my managers.

I knew the technology inside out, so I looked pretty respectable for the people in the Virtual box. They thought I was some billionaire who had many secrets. It was funny to know that people took me for some business guru, but I was just a regular guy who knew the technology and biology pretty well. Many people asked me simple questions, and I gave them my simple answers. After all, I was trying to be nice. I wanted to keep my profile low, so I didn't engage in big ventures like Apple presentations, Microsoft meetings, Tesla conventions, BMW parties or any other major convention of the big 500 companies in the Virtual Box.

You know the real world has S&P 500, but the Virtual box has VR 500 and that is a million times bigger than its S&P 500 predecessor. There were stories that Max Styles, the CEO of Virtual Box, was buying properties all over the world and that he was the biggest property and landowner ever. I hoped those were only rumors, because those kinds of accusations could get him a really terrible reputation and affect his public image.

One night I was driving home from work down an alley in my old Tesla when I saw a man on the street. He seemed lonely and sad. He was obviously homeless and nearby was a pizza place. I guessed he could use a snack so I went to the pizza place and bought a pizza and some coca cola for him. He seemed happy when I gave them to him. His eyes shone brightly and he thanked me and blessed me. That was one of the most beautiful moments of my life. I felt good because I had helped someone and it gave me the idea that I wanted to feel that buzz again.

Next day I went to see Simone.

She looked at me and smiled. "Hello there, handsome."

"Hello there, beautiful," I replied. "Maybe we should get something to eat?"

"Yeah, sure," she said. "What would you like?"

"Let's get some of that tasty Asian food that you like," I suggested and she smiled again.

"Yeah, we should definitely get that."

We went to the nearest Asian place where we got the best sushi and Chinese food ever.

I smiled and kissed Simone. Her lips were soft and warm. There was something about her look when she smiled and when she gave me a kiss. She always seemed to make it unforgettable and I knew that I would love her and make her happy for all time.

We cycled down to the beach on bikes, smiling and having fun all the way. When we arrived we relaxed for a while near the beach, listening to the waves crashing on the sand and enjoying the sights and smells.

Then we took our bikes on to the sandy dunes and gazed at the sea. It was an amazing time; we kissed and smiled a lot and the view from the top of the sandy dunes was amazing. After some time gazing at the sea we went for a swim in the water. She looked even more beautiful with the salty water cascading over her body. When we came back to the dunes we kissed again and lay in one another's arms, happy in each other's company.

We had a wonderful time together and that evening, as we looked into each other's eyes, we talked about the things that were important to us. We stayed until it got dark and then cycled back again. Our love grew with every minute we were together and we had become inseparable. We were happy together, and we would be together and nothing and no one could stop us.

That night we spent together. We were like two parts of something that had no beginning and no end. The two of us were like one. Every small freckle on her body was pure gold and I couldn't stop looking at her all night. Somehow we both knew that we were meant to be together.

Next day I made her a breakfast. It wasn't anything fancy, just some toast, eggs and coffee, but she appreciated the gesture.

"I'm so hungry," she said as she walked into the kitchen.

"This will be tasty," I promised.

She ate the whole thing and I gave her some fruit juice and she loved the taste of that too.

"Did you enjoy the food?" I asked, as she mopped up the last of it from her plate.

She nodded. "Yes it was very good."

I kissed her and smiled.

"I'm glad that you liked it."

We both wanted to go somewhere to relax, so we went for walk in the city. A few people recognized her and wanted a photo. She smiled and agreed. She was really famous and it could be uncomfortable for me at times, but somehow I got the hang of it. We went to a great pizza place with holographic screens and robot waiters. It was crazy how quickly they made us a great pizza. We loved eating that pizza and every time I looked at her, the smile on her face brightened the room. There was something mesmerizing about her. She had something that moved people. She was a person with a big heart and a warm smile.

When our stomachs were full, we went for a walk. We talked and had fun and I tickled her. We went to the port where we saw a small bar near the bay. We chose a table and sat down. The warm wind from the bay ran through her hair and she looked amazing. We ordered some drinks and relaxed, talking about everything and nothing at all. She liked my stories and I liked everything that she told me about herself. She had an interesting life story. After her mother's death she had depression and her father enrolled her in the Virtual Sandbox program. After seeing his daughter's speedy recovery in the virtual world, her father kept her inside a cocoon and visited her every week to see how she was feeling.

"I don't remember the real world anymore," she said sadly. "It's been so long since I walked on my own feet. I don't think I would remember how to walk in the real world now."

"The real world is very different," I conceded. "Here the time flies and there is always an adventure behind every corner. The real world is hard; it has many ways to keep people on their knees. Alcohol, drugs, cigarettes are all banned in the virtual world, but they thrive in the real one. People get addicted and their lives crumble. I have seen many people broken and destroyed by drugs and other substances; they are not people anymore, now they are more like zombies. The most terrible thing you can get into in the real world is drugs or alcohol."

"Why do people choose these horrible things?" she asked.

"The same reason we are here now in the Virtual world," I replied. "They want to escape from reality."

"But that's terrible." She seemed really saddened by that.

"Yes, it is. Drug or alcohol addiction is horrible," I admitted.

"How do these people get help?" she asked.

"Many don't," I said, "but some lucky ones do. Many addicts die from overdoses or other diseases like aids."

"My God," she gasped. "Reality is terrible."

"Yes, sometimes it is. But, you know, I still like reality," I said.

"Why?" She seemed utterly shocked that I could like something that could bring such misery to so many people.

"I have real friends there," I explained. "Friends who have my back, and I got theirs. I have people that I love in reality. My parents are wonderful, my relatives are great and I can trust them all."

"I have friends too," Simone said, almost indignantly.

"Yes, but can you trust them? Have you checked them out in a difficult situation? Do you know their motives?"

"I think I do."

"It's good if you have real friends," I said, "but if you have fake friends, it's worse than having no friends at all. Some people smile in your face when they have a knife behind your back. I hate those kinds of people."

"I really have a few friends I can trust," she insisted.

I smiled. " That's good then. Cherish them always."

We walked on the beach. We talked some more and took some photos and had a great time, kissing and laughing at the gulls that swooped and dived above our heads. She giggled when I tickled her and liked the touch of my hands. We were inseparable and it felt like we were people who met each other after thousands of years of solitude. We lay down on the beach to relax and looked up at the clouds.

"What is the best thing in the real world?" she asked.

I had to think for a minute. "Lots of things, but I guess that the best thing is to have children."

"I see," she said. "Do you want to have children?"

"I don't know," I admitted, "I've never really thought about it."

"Why not?" she asked. "Have you never loved somebody so much that you wanted to have children with them?"

"There was one time," I said.

"Oh, tell me about it," she pleaded.

"It's complicated." The truth was that it was hard to talk about.

"What was complicated?"

"I had trust issues with that person. Maybe I was wrong; maybe I just needed to trust her."

"Why didn't you trust her?"

"I don't know," I said, "It's complicated, like I said, maybe it's my fault."

"Do you want to go back to her?" Simone asked and her question shook me.

"No. It's in the past. If you think about the past, you mess up your future. You can't come back and change the past, its life."

Then she asked the question that really sealed the deal for me. "Do you want children with me?"

I turned my head and kissed her. The kiss was refreshing and warm; her soft lips reminding me of something sweet. I felt something I had forgotten a long time ago, something that I held dear, something that made me forget my past and look to the future once more.

She smiled back at me.

"Does this mean yes?"

"Yes, it does," I said.

"I want to meet in the real world with you," Simone suddenly announced.

"Me too," I said. "But for now it isn't possible."

"Why?"

"It's hard to explain. I don't know if I should tell you."

"Come on, tell me," she pleaded.

"I tried it and failed," I said.

"Try again," she said with a sparkle in her eyes, "but try better this time."

"I will fail again," I insisted.

"So fail better until you get to me," she said.

I sighed. "It's not that simple."

"It is simple, just think of something."

"You're in a secure location, I can't get there," I replied.

She was silent for a moment but she was soon back at her optimistic best again. "Don't worry, you will think of something."

"I hope so," I said.

"I know you will," she said confidently.

Through all this time, despite all our happiness, her mind faded a few times and I knew I had to do something. This fading of consciousness really bothered me. Something was really wrong in the virtual world, but I just didn't know what.

When I returned home, I became very nervous. I feared for Simone's health and I didn't know how I could help her. This feeling of helplessness bothered me to the core. I was anxious and didn't know what to do. My love for her burned deep within me and I knew I had to do something about this fading of her consciousness. There are so many people in the world and so many problems, but I saw only her in my mind. I was obsessed somehow and I didn't sleep at all that night. My mind was full of thoughts and ideas of how I could get her out and help her. But that sleepless night didn't help at all in the end because the ideas in my head were immature or foolish.

Next day I was tired as hell. That sleepless night got to me and I went to see my friends to get my mind straight. We went to the bar and soon they knew that something was wrong.

"Something is wrong with you John," said Mark. "You look like a zombie."

"What's wrong John?" asked Luke. "We are all friends. You can tell us."

"It's nothing," I lied. "I just had a sleepless night."

"Something is wrong," said James. "For the last few months you've been flying like you had wings. We don't recognize you. First you're funny, smart and happy and now you're like a dead man."

"Did you do drugs or something?" asked Mark.

"Don't be ridiculous," I snapped. "Are you crazy?"

"We can help, we care about you," Luke implored.

I couldn't tell them about what I had done. It was too risky to get them involved and it was something I had to work out for myself. "It's something personal," I said. "I just don't want to tell you yet."

"Okay John, we get it," said Luke, "but don't get in trouble. Something tells me this isn't a simple problem that you are in. But it's your choice if you want to keep it a secret."

"I will tell you in time," I replied. "I just need time to figure it out. That's all."

"Hope it's nothing illegal?" Luke muttered.

"Don't worry. It's not drugs, not weapon sales and not human trafficking," I joked.

That seemed to lighten the moment a bit and they all visibly relaxed a bit.

"Okay, it's not the evil triad," said Mark. "That's good news at least. We have to stay off those three things, because it only gets people killed."

"Or puts you to jail for life," James chipped in.

"You are right there," laughed Luke.

"Okay, let's get some beers in guys. I'm fed up with all this talk about death and prison."

"Good idea," said Mark. "It's your round anyway."

I bought some more beers for us all and we ended up having a great time talking and relaxing together. We talked about the future and remembered old jokes and funny stories. After a few beers and a great time together we went home. My old Tesla did the taxi job that night and when we said our goodbyes and parted Mark whispered to me.

"John, I don't know what is going with you, but you better fix your stuff. You know we are your friends and you can count on us."

"I know, Mark. I know," I replied.

"See you soon John," he winked. "Be safe and don't get into any trouble."

"I will, Mark. Bye."

When I got home, the only thing in my mind was how to help Simone. I was close to running out of options, but my head was working pretty well. I hoped I would think of something and that the idea would be good. I fell on the bed, tired and frustrated. My legs felt like stone and my hands were heavy like blocks of concrete. I knew I needed to rest, and I needed it badly.

The next day I was refreshed and almost immediately I connected to Virtual Box and met Simone.

When I saw her all my problems seemed to melt away. "Hello," I said.

"Hello there," she responded. Her eyes were glittering like stars. "Come on, I need to show you something."

She took me by the hand and to a nice shop with wonderful dresses in the windows.

"I want to go out tonight," she stated. "Will you accompany me?"

"Sure," I said. "Where do you want to go?"

"There is a nice place in town. I want to relax and have a ball."

"Okay, sounds good to me." I was up for just about anything to take my mind off things.

"Yes, and I want you to meet my dad," she added.

"Wait a minute," I stammered. "Are you sure? Is he going to like me? It's really fast."

She kissed me and smiled.

"Don't worry, it will be fine. He doesn't bite."

"I'm not sure about that," I replied, a bit unsure, but Simone had made her mind up.

"Just be yourself," she laughed. "He's going to love you."

The whole day I was thinking about meeting Simone's father. I heard he was a tough business owner who had lots of interests in the Virtual box. I was a little scared of him. He seemed to be a strong and determined man. I hoped he would like me.

I met Simone the next day. She seemed happy and excited.

"My dad agreed to meet you," she gushed. "He will be in New York tomorrow."

"Okay," I said. "That's nice."

My hands were shaking behind my back, but I didn't want her to know that I was scared.

Soon she was back to her usual self. "Let's go somewhere. I'm starving."

"What do you have in mind?" I asked.

"How about we grab some sushi?" she suggested.

I said, "Okay, that sounds good to me," and before long we were in a nice sushi bar, with holographic screens and a large menu. There were all kinds of sushi, we just couldn't pick one, so we ordered a plate of four different types. The accompanying sauce was fantastic and we really enjoyed our dinner. Simone loved that place.

"Look," she said suddenly, pointing at a large screen. "There's my music video. They probably got my music rights."

There was something innocent about her in that moment and I couldn't take my eyes off her. "You know you are beautiful," I said and leaned in for a kiss.

There was something about her. I looked into her eyes and that smile lit the entire room. I smiled back at her and softly kissed her lips again. Her warm hands ran down my face. I kissed them and smiled at her. She smiled back at me and I kissed her again.

We felt like we were the only people in the world because we didn't care about others. We loved each other more than life itself; we were inseparable, like fish and the sea. We wanted to go somewhere nice, so we went back to the beach. Down there, among the sand and the sea, she looked even more beautiful, her hair shone in the sun and her smile was fabulous. We sat down and looked at the horizon; the view was amazing. That atmosphere, that view, and Simone next to me, was the most wonderful thing in my life and all I needed in that moment. She sat closer to me; I hugged her and felt her warm body next to mine. I kissed her on the cheek; she smiled and looked into my eyes. We were destined to be together. I held her hand while gazing at the broad horizon.

We stayed there for hours and later we headed for home. I left her at her place and then returned to my work in the real world.

I made some modifications for cryogenic cocoons, fixed some work I had to do and was eager for my meeting with Simone's dad the following day. I was apprehensive about it because I didn't know how Simone's father would react to me. Would he know that I was someone who secretly connected to the Virtual Box? I heard he was a tough guy, and he had lots of businesses, so I didn't want to come across as some sort of screw up.

The next day I didn't want to get out of my bed. I knew I had that meeting in the evening and it scared me to my bones. After all, I had never been in that sort of situation before and it was all new to me. Somehow I managed to pull myself together and got to work and connected.

Simone came to pick me up.

"You seem nervous somehow, she said. "Don't worry, everything will be fine. Just relax and it will all work out."

"I hope so," I said weakly.

"Don't be scared. My father doesn't bite," she laughed. "He just wants to get to know you. He won't interrogate you; he's not one of those people."

We talked all day and she did her best to calm me down. After some time she managed to make me feel more relaxed about things and I felt more comfortable. She told me the things that shouldn't talk about with her father and what he liked and disliked. She made me comfortable, and gradually I felt more confident and ready for the meeting.

That day flew by so fast and finally Simone and I had to make our way to the restaurant where her father would be waiting for us. My nerves had returned but Simone was always next to me.

Then I saw him. He was a tall, strong, muscular man who looked like he didn't suffer fools gladly. I reached out and offered him a hand and when he shook it I could feel the power in it.

" Hello, John, it's good to finally meet you," he said. It was an amiable greeting and he sounded like he meant it.

"Nice to meet you too, sir," I replied, as confidently as I could.

Simone and her dad exchanged greetings and a kiss on the cheek.

"So John, how was your day?" her dad asked.

"It was great," I said. "I managed to spend time with Simone."

"Yeah we had a great day," Simone added.

"Good," he said as he examined the menu. "I had a few interesting meetings with the board today. We are planning a new software launch of the sandbox cocoon pods."

"Will you launch after the New Year or before?" I asked.

"Why do you want to know?" he responded, suddenly seeming suspicious.

"After the New Year, the company will raise taxes for the new software," I explained.

His eyebrows raised just a fraction. "Really. I didn't know that. You have a very smart boyfriend, Simone."

"Thank you," smiled Simone. "I know he is smart."

"That could save my company millions," he said. "You might have really helped me out, John."

"No problem," I replied. "I just shared the information."

"I'll tell my team to work harder and wrap up the deal before the New Year," he stated.

He seemed pleased with the idea that he could save a lot of money and it helped break the ice with him a bit. After perusing the menu for a while he spoke again.

"So John, what are your plans for the future?"

"He's just looking for new opportunities," Simone offered. "Are you, John?" he asked.

"Yes, there is one thing I'm looking into right now, but I can't tell you all the details yet," I said.

He smiled. "Great. A man with secrets. I like that. Work in silence, let your success be your noise."

"What do you mean? I asked. "I don't understand."

"It's a quote that I like," he replied. "I think it's from Frank Ocean."

"I like quotes too," I said. "My favorite is You change your life by changing your heart, by Max Lucado."

"It's beautiful John," Simone purred.

"Yes, it really is," her father agreed.

We ordered some soups and grilled chicken. The food was great and the robot servers did their job pretty well. It was a wonderful evening and we laughed and joked a lot, talked about the future and generally had a good time together. My deep knowledge about technologies and biology really impressed Simone's father and I gradually became more and more relaxed in his company.

"You know that it's the first time in my life I met such a smart person, John," Simone's father enthused. "You know a lot of things about the Virtual Box. You will really go far, I'm sure of it."

"Thank you sir," I said. "I certainly hope that I will."

We eventually said our goodbyes after a delicious meal and returned to Simone's place. She took off her coat and looked into my eyes like never before. I leaned to kiss her. Her soft lips touched mine. I hugged her and pressed her body closer to mine. My lips ran over her neck and shoulders. She kissed me on the lips and we sank deep into each other. Her lips were like cherries, soft and gentle. I liked every touch. I looked into her eyes and they were beautiful like never before. She looked amazing. My hands over her skin and she lay on the bed.

I got closer to her and we kissed like there was no tomorrow. We stayed like that until midnight. She was enjoying our time together and wanted more and more from me, while did my best to make her happy and comfortable.

We didn't let go of each other that entire night. Her lips and her kisses made me wild. Her body was wonderful and she knew her body and emotions pretty well. Her breath was restless and intense. She loved my every touch. Every part of her body was tingling from my touches and we couldn't stop loving each other throughout the whole night. Her body and soul were fused to me and her mind was dedicated to my soft touches on her body.

I saw her on the balcony next morning; she was smoking something. She had my shirt on and looked damn sexy. I walked closer to her, hugged her, and kissed her.

"Good morning, sexy," she said in that soft and silky voice of hers.

"Good morning, love," I responded.

"You were wonderful last night," she purred.

"You were too," I said.

"You seem to know all the right buttons to push, and I loved it."

"What will we do now?" I asked.

"Now we will enjoy our perfect moment together," she said.

"Why do you like me?" I asked. I guess it was that old insecurity coming out again.

"Your smile, I guess," she replied. "You have a beautiful smile."

"Come on? Really?" I asked. Could it be that simple?

"Yeah you do, you just don't know it yet."

I smiled and looked into her eyes; she smiled and kissed me. The kiss was soft and gentle. Then I sunk into her lips and hugged her like never before. Her body was warm and sensuous. She was like a flower that bloomed in a man's hands.

"What's the plan for today?" she asked later.

"Eat and relax," I said. That was our usual one.

"It's a good plan," she teased.

"I know it is," I said. "I thought it up all by myself."

She laughed at that but then became serious again. "John, what inspires you?" she asked.

"You." "I know that. What else?"

"I never thought about it."

"There has to be something that makes you wake up in the morning. For me, it's music," she said.

I thought for a moment. "I like to help people. I guess."

"That's an appropriate answer," she laughed. "I think you are a good person."

" I hope I am," I replied. "But you are also a good person, Simone. You make people happy when they hear your songs. You inspire people and that is good."

"Thank you," she replied. "You're so nice."

"But there must be something that you want for yourself?" I asked.

"I don't know, really," she replied. "I will tell you when I find out. I think I have everything I need right here."

We looked up at the sky from the balcony. It was a beautiful shade of blue that you just didn't get in the real world. It was almost completely clear, with only few clouds scattered around and I realized that this day was the most beautiful one of my life. I was thrilled and Simone was really happy with me. I wanted that this day would last forever.

"Do you want some coffee or tea?" I asked. "I will make it for you."

" Yeah, sure. Tea would be nice," she replied.

I made some tea and put some lemon into it. We sat down on the balcony again and looked into the sky. She sipped the tea and her smile brightened the room and could have broken even a stone heart. I couldn't resist kissing her and the fresh lemon tea from her mouth tasted really sweet. My lips ended up on her neck. Her soft skin made me go wild with desire. The touches of her warm hands felt like butterflies fluttering over my skin. We had actual love, and it was amazing. We had a special connection that bonded us together. We had each other, and it was all that really mattered. Looking at that sky and those clouds made us understand we needed each other more than anything. After all, we were perfect for each other.

After some time we got hungry and wanted to eat somewhere. Virtual world had a broad choice of restaurants and diners. We thought to try something new. There was a place that made exceptional pizzas. It was famous in the whole Virtual box. All the famous people liked to visit that place, because it had a great atmosphere and many people visited it again and again. Something was attracting people back for another byte of their pizza.

We sat down to have a byte of a fresh and tasty pizza. We had our eyes on the pizza with chicken. A robot server rushed in to take an order from us. He was so funny and original that we couldn't stop laughing at his humor. Those robots were really cute and that was maybe the ingredient of success in this pizza place. Someone prepared our pizza really quick and soon our mouths were full of tasty slices of a wonderful meal. Somehow time flew by really quickly and we had great time, but soon it was time for me to return to the real world once more and write a status report for my managers. I had to do this job every quarter, and it required a lot of concentration. I said goodbye to Simone and promised to return as soon as I could.

When I got back to my desk at the company I missed Simone a lot. Her soft kisses and warm skin were in my head all the time. I couldn't concentrate and do my work because Simone's face was always with me in my thoughts. It was really hard to get on with what I had to do, but I had to write that status report. I gathered all my strength and somehow wrote that paper.

When I was done I sat in my Tesla and ordered my car to take me home. I fell into bed like a dead man. I could only think about Simone and nothing else. Finally, I fell asleep.

The next morning I woke up fresh and new. I got to work quickly and got connected to the Virtual box. I then called Simone as fast as I could. She came to our meeting place with a cute look, wearing a white shirt and a short schoolgirl skirt that would make any man jealous if they saw her with me. Her sexy look inspired me to give her a long, passionate kiss. She smiled and took my hand. She was excited to see me as always and took me to an airport. The plane was waiting for us on the tarmac and it was an ultra-modern one that I had never seen before.

"Where are we going?" I asked.

"It's a secret," she smiled. "Trust me."

"Okay," I agreed. "You've got my interest already."

"Good," she replied as she climbed the steps. "You are gonna love it."

The plane was luxurious; it had all the things you could imagine. The stewardess offered us a glass of wine as we settled into our seats and Simone looked happy and excited.

"Okay," I said as I sipped the wine. "Where are we heading?"

"It's a surprise," she repeated

I could barely take my eyes off her. "You look really sexy in that schoolgirl outfit," I smiled.

Simone giggled. "You noticed then? Thank you. I tried."

She looked so attractive in it and her long silky legs drove me crazy. There was something about her that drove men wild. But here she was, only interested in me.

The flight wasn't too long and soon I could feel the sensation that we were losing some altitude.

"So are you ready for the surprise?" she asked as the flight seemed to be coming to an end.

"I think so," I smiled.

"Look through the window," she said.

I did as she said and could see clean beaches with small cabins close to each other. The view was like it had been taken from a magazine. It was something amazing. We could see beautiful, pristine water and I recognized it almost at once as the Maldives. Virtual world was really magnificent; it looked if it has copied all the best parts of the real world and left only the bad ones behind.

"And this is our destination," said Simone as we descended further.

I was blown away. "Wow, it's beautiful," I said. It truly was.

"It will be ours for a few days," said Simone.

"Great, I love it. How did you come up with this?" I asked.

I have a head on my shoulders don't I?

"Yes. The surprise is wonderful."

We landed at a small airport on the island. She took my hand and invited me to a house near the beach. You could see the beautiful water from windows. She sat down on the bed and smiled at me. I leaned in to kiss her. Her warm cherry lips filled my mouth and my tongue started playing with hers. My lips explored her neck and shoulders. She was excited, and her breath was quick and restless. She lay down on the bed and I continued passionately kissing her. Slowly, my hands ran through her legs. She looked really sexy in her schoolgirl uniform. My mind was fully dedicated to her. I wanted her to feel my kisses all over her body. I sunk into her beautiful lips and refused to let go. My tongue was playing games and made her excited. She was the woman of my dreams, and I was the man of hers. She knew I would be faithful to her and never leave her. Our passion grew every single moment. Every part of her body felt magnificent. I wanted to give her the best of me. My touches made her feel wanted and desired. My hands were all over her wonderful body. Her desire for me grew more every moment when we were together. My love for her was undeniable. My soft touches made her more and more excited. My kisses made her go wild. Her body was like a masterpiece of art and could make anyone go crazy for her. Her breath was getting slower and more intense. My kisses were running all over her body and my soft touches excited her. We couldn't let go of each other's bodies. We were like one united body. That night made us even crazier for each other if that was even possible.

Next morning I woke up in wonderful spirits. I saw her bathing in the water. She looked beautiful, as always. Her whole body looked amazing in the fresh water and went to her and kissed her on the neck. She turned and sunk into my lips.

"Good morning," I whispered.

"Good morning, beautiful," she responded.

"You look amazing," I said.

"You do too," she replied.

"How are you feeling?" I asked.

"I feel great," she said. "But there is something strange. Sometimes I lack concentration."

I was immediately concerned. "Has it happened before?"

"It has, but rarely. Now it's happening more often. Something is wrong."

She sounded worried and I hated hearing the uncertainty in her voice.

"Don't worry," I said. "I'll think of something."

I left the Virtual Box and went to see my friends. I needed their help because they were people I could trust. I knew I couldn't help Simone without them and I was now ready to explain why I had changed. Simone was the most important thing now and I knew that I had to act to help her before it was too late.

We met at the bar, and I told them everything. They seemed surprised that I could have kept a secret like this for so long, but they agreed to help me.

"Okay," said Luke. "We have to get inside the system and find out what Simone's condition is."

"You have to get me the data," James added. "It's vitally important that we know what is happening with her brain."

Mark's security brain was working overtime already "Do you remember that security flaw, Luke?"

"Yes," said Luke. "I remember that. It's written in the kernel and we could use it."

"It sounds good," I said. "But how we will get the data?"

"You can use Kali Linux," said Mark. "It's a small operating system used by hackers to extract sensitive data from company computers. But it is dangerous, the system could spot you."

"We have to get the data as soon as possible," said Luke with urgency in his voice. "We don't know how her brain is reacting to the Virtual Box."

"Okay," I said, with a new determination. "I will download Kali and will put it on a flash drive. Then I will connect to the terminal with Kali and extract the data."

"You need to extract the data safely, without running red flags on the system," Mark advised.

"Can you write software for that?" I asked.

"I can probably write something with Python," he said.

It was in those few minutes that I realized what my friends were doing and willing to risk for me.

"You are good friends," I said.

I just hope you are right John," said Mark. "I don't want to hack a corporate network just to find out that you are wrong."

"He could be right," said Luke. "The brainwaves are a complex system. Without solving problems in the real world, she might be just fading away."

"Okay, it's decided," said Mark. "We want to help you John; I just hope you're not leading us into trouble we can't handle.

"John is our friend," said Luke with a smile. "We have to help him, no matter what."

John was nervous when he entered his workplace. There was a terminal near the main gate. Every time the clock strike twelve the terminal was empty, because everybody went to eat. I knew that and when twelve struck, I connected to it. The computer was old and bulky, but it was the only place without any security cameras near it. It scared me a little, but I knew I had to get the information. It was really important. The fate of Simone depended on this and I knew that if I didn't get the information, something terrible might happen.

The drive connected, it had the Kali Linux logo on the drive and I launched the program. Soon the data was slowly extracted from the database. It scared me that somebody might see me, but I had to finish my shift so as not to arouse any suspicions. After that I went straight to Luke.

"Here is the drive," I said, handing it to him.

He quickly examined the date and his brow furrowed as he took in what he was viewing.

"Do you see this?"

"What?" "Those patterns. They are not normal."

"What do you mean?" I asked.

Luke pointed at some lines. "You must understand that these waves are becoming more and more distorted. We need to get her out."

"How are we going to do that?" I asked.

"Simple," said Luke. "We get in the complex and get her out."

It didn't sound very simple. "It's a protected complex," I reminded him. "It's not possible."

Luke smiled at me. "I have doctor clearance, remember?"

"Yes, but how we are going to get past the guards?"

"That's the hard part," Luke admitted. "Mark will have to hack the system. There is no other way."

"It may be easy enough to get in, but how we will get out?" I asked.

"The New Year's ball on Trinity," suggested Luke.

I scratched my chin as I digested the idea. "Yes, it might work. The entire world will be watching it and even the guards won't understand that it's not only a drill when we get the cocoon with Simone out. That ball happens only once a year."

"Do cocoons have internet?" Luke asked.

"No," I said. "But I can try to connect to the global net with a modem."

"Could you really do that? Will it be safe?" Luke was skeptical.

"We did it in university," I said. "It's quite simple, and you only need a satellite modem."

"Okay," Luke agreed. "Mark will have to get us in and out.

You will install the modem and I will look at her medical condition. Where will we hide?"

"I think we can thrust James with that," said Mark.

"Really?" I asked.

"James was a trauma recovery specialist back in the days when I was learning to be a doctor," Luke explained. "He was pretty good and he could keep a secret for a long time."

"He also works in security of the Virtual Box servers and he can keep the information hidden for some time," Mark reminded me. "Simone will need time to recover and learn to walk again once she is out."

When I got back inside the Virtual Box, I hugged Simone. She smiled and kissed me as hard and as passionate as she had ever done. I wanted her to be happy more than anything in the world and so I told her the plan. She was dubious at first, but when I explained that we would have help from my friends and that they all had their own particular set of skills she soon accepted that this was her only chance.

We waited for the New Year like two lovers waited for the day of their marriage. We knew we couldn't mess up, because it was too dangerous for Simone to stay any longer in the Virtual world. I tried to keep her calm as we waited and she did manage to relax a bit. Days flew by quickly. I knew that when we were together nothing else mattered to us. Our time together was the most important thing and we always wanted it to be special, even now as we waited to know what our fates would become.

We went to the parks where birdsongs made us feel alive and whole again; we visited the seashore and all the beauty it brought to our lives. We were like one mind, fused together; she was the only woman that mattered to me. Her eyes sparkled and her smile lit up each day. I knew we had to be strong and wait for the New Year and the Trinity spaceship and then we would have a chance to be together in the real world.

Days went by like water flowing through a river. We had to be careful and not to talk to anyone about our secret to escape.

Simone's coordination became weaker as the days passed, and we knew we had to do something about it. It was almost the day when we had to fly to the virtual open space and reach Trinity in the lower orbit.

We knew we had to be careful just to be safe. The space pods were launching from Canada and everybody wanted to be on board. Mark had managed to get us hacked tickets, and luckily the receptionist was fooled by them. She also recognized Simone and got us the best seats available.

When it launched, we experienced virtual launch dizziness, but it was only temporary and soon we would be where it mattered most.

"How are you? Is everything fine?" I asked.

"I'm fine," Simone assured me. "Just relax. You have to know that I love you."

I smiled at her. "I love you too."

"It's important that you stay with me," she insisted.

"When you sing, we will disconnect you from the system, you may experience dizziness," I said. "When that happens, go to your room and lay down. We will get you out of the system as soon as possible."

"Will it be dangerous?" she asked.

"No," I reassured her. "We will connect you with a modem to one of the Elon's satellites. You just have to be careful and wait for my signal until we can leave the cocoon farm."

"What will the signal be?"

"Three short bumps on the cocoon, then one long one and three

short ones again."

"That's SOS in Morse code," she said.

"Yes it is," I said. "It's easier for you to remember. Now, let's enjoy the party. After all, we are guests at Trinity."

"Yes," she smiled, "we will. It's important for us to be as discreet as possible. Do you play poker?"

"No I don't."

"Why not?"

I laughed. "Because no matter how you play, the casino always wins."

"Do you drink?"

"No I don't," I said. "People do stupid things when they are drunk."

"How we are going to have fun then?" she asked, exasperated.

"We don't," I replied. "We have to be careful."

"So what we are going to do?"

"Simple," I said. "We will have a chat with interesting people, look around the ship, and enjoy food and people from different places. I heard there is a park in the ship, we could see exotic animals and have fun while gazing at the stars. Enjoy the simple things, Simone. They are the best."

After walking for some time through the ship we felt comfort in the company of each other and that was all that mattered. The ship was amazing it had a roof of tempered glass where you could only see open space beyond. They had decorated the ship with golden elements and 19th century furniture and lamps. It looked like it had been made before the world wars. The beauty of the ship was magnificent and there was nothing like it anywhere else. It had all the wonders of a truly amazing creation.

It was gone midnight. The time had seemed to slip by without us noticing it and now it was time for our plan to swing into action. We had no idea if it would work or not but I knew that if I was ever going to save Simone from certain death that I had to act and we had to do it now.

The New Year party on Trinity had given us the perfect distraction for our plan to be implemented and Luke, Mark and James had been meticulous in their preparations that would hopefully see us safely out of the virtual world and back in the real one where I could take care of Simone for the rest of our lives.

I looked at my watch. It was now or never. Simone was standing with her back to me, gazing at the stars. She had never looked more at peace than now and I wished that I could have let her stand there for hours, just soaking up that amazing view.

But we couldn't linger. We had to move. It was time to go. It was time to leave this fake world far behind us and return to reality, where we could live like real people once more and not in some box where everything was perfect.

That was the ironic thing about the virtual world. Its perfection was its downfall. It was the thing that made it imperfect if you can understand that and if it makes any sense.

It was a place where nothing went wrong and where everything was always going to be just fine, so long as you had the cash that would let you live there for eternity. But even that had its drawbacks as we had discovered and the longer I had remained immersed in its fake beauty, the more I wanted nothing but to return to the imperfect world of reality, where I could have a beer with my friends, criticize war and famine and poverty and the million other things that were wrong in the world.

The one thing I had come to understand was that no amount of fake perfection would ever be enough to cure the planet's ills. It was okay for a short visit. It was fine if you were fabulously wealthy and could forget the world's problems, but that was as far as it went.

The problems were always there. They may always be there. We may never rid ourselves of them, no matter how hard we try. But I knew now that striving to make the world a better place in reality was better than building something that was simply unattainable for billions and which would never contribute anything other than a dazzling opportunity to be something you weren't.

Simone turned to me. It was almost as if she had read my mind.

"Is it time?" she asked. Her voice was weakening, even as she spoke.

"Yes it is," I smiled back at her.

I took her hand and led her away from that view in a trillion, back to the glass elevator that would take us to the floor where we could escape from this madness.

As she walked I took one last, longing, backward glance at the spectacle. It truly was stunning with the billions of stars shimmering in the darkness, and for one brief moment I was tempted to stay a bit longer, just for that.

But I knew it was time and I forced myself to look away. I would never return to the virtual world ever again; of that I was now certain. My future was with Simone, in reality, where we could marry, have children, argue, see the real world, meet with our real friends, party, go on vacations, have fun and live.

All we had to do was trust...

Epilogue

It has been a year since I stood at that window on the Trinity. A year in which I somehow managed to extricate the love of my life from a potentially life-threatening situation and brought her out of the virtual world and into the real one.

The plan worked to perfection and we brought her out and she went to live with James for a while. We knew the authorities would be right behind us; there was no way we were going to evade them for ever and the only solution was that I took the rap while she stayed hidden.

It wasn't easy. Saying goodbye to Simone when I knew she was still very weak and fragile and then going to my apartment to await that knock on the door was the hardest thing I ever did. But she understood and she knew that this was the only way. James was under the radar enough for us to leave her with him. The second apartment he had (one which he had bought from money he had been left) was unknown to anyone and it was perfect.

In the end it wasn't the FBI or Interpol or even the Virtual Box cops who go to me – it was work. Corporate had figured out that I had been involved because there was no way I could completely hide what I had been doing, and the very day I returned to work they descended on me.

That was tough. That first meeting with them last five hours and they did almost everything they could to make me give her up. They threatened me, cajoled me, offered me incentives and downright lied. They threatened to sack me on the spot, told me they would have my parents evicted from their apartment and said they would make sure I never worked again in anything other than a menial job.

When I didn't crack they changed tack and offered me a promotion if I told them where Simone was and how I had managed to get her out. When that didn't work they offered me cash; more money than I could have earned in two lifetimes.

And when that didn't work they let me leave. I was suspended for a month, pending an investigation. That was extended to three months and then to six. All the while I was suspended they watched my apartment, day and night. I couldn't leave without being followed. I couldn't phone Simone for fear that my call would be traced. It was hell.

But towards the end of that sixth month from hell a new hope emerged. Luke had been keeping a close eye on Simone and her condition and as she gradually improved he used his notes to write a paper on her.

That was explosive. Virtual Box was shown up for what it was and from then on in it was game over. No matter what they did things gradually got worse for them as more and more people started to come forward with their experiences.

Others 'escaped' from it as well and before long the whole concept was shaken to its core. Before long Max Styles was on the ropes and the only plan he had was to try to wrest control of the Virtual Sandbox from Elon.

With help of the Russian Mafia he set out to destroy Elon in a spectacular show of strength such as the world had never seen from an individual before. He launched rockets at Mars, knowing that Elon was still on the planet, in the hope of eliminating him once and for all.

With Elon out of the way there would have been nothing standing in Styles' path and he would have gained total control of trillions of dollars-worth of assets. But his plan failed.

Elon was already alerted to what was going on back on Earth and had secretly been building a plasma cannon which was used to knock out the missiles long before they reached him.

With his last throw of the dice now failed, Styles was finished. He was arrested, his assets were seized and he was put in prison for the rest of his days for an act of interplanetary terrorism.

When Elon returned to Earth he discovered that Luke had written his paper and offered him a job as the Chief Medical Officer of Virtual Box. Then, in an act of supreme generosity, he made the Virtual Sandbox free for everyone, achieving the greatest feat of mankind, the eradication of poverty once and for all.

For James and Mark life is also pretty good. Mark now has his own company and is married to a great woman. James is famous the world over and lives an incredible life of luxury that can only be dreamt of.

And me? I'm standing here, nervous as hell, waiting for Simone. My friends and family are all here and the scene is set. It has been a hell of a ride and a long year of waiting but finally we are here and ready to take the next step on our whirlwind adventure. I'm about to marry the most wonderful woman I ever met and we are going to spend the rest of our lives together.

In reality.

THE END

The virtual world seemed endless, but our world wasn't. We had our limitations. We were still mortal people, we suffered from the same problems as others: problems like pain, loss, insecurities, belonging to someone who needed us the most, sickness, wealth, all of this mattered when we were here and now, not sunk in our dream worlds, that we wanted to reach and forgot the really important things, like our loved ones who needed us the most.

Somehow everything that we reached didn't matter so much when we encountered our world of insecurities. We must be better, we must do better, if we don't, we will be nothing more than the echoes of our past. We must build safe homes, we must create safety for us and our families, and we must create a world better than we had yesterday, because if we don't, we will be nothing more than the echoes of emptiness in the endless space of our past. Someone who doesn't value what he has is bound to lose it. If you could choose to be anyone you have to choose yourself. Not someone with Botox, fake lips or implants, but someone who loves you for who you are.

If you want to work out, work out, if you want to change yourself little by little, do that, but it shouldn't be some drastic change that could ruin your health. You have to know that after all, small things matter. Great people always start small and reach their goals little by little. You can do it too. By small changes you make the big change and small work, like cleaning a room, will always be important work for anyone who is interested in helping his family or others. Nobody seems to realize how making small changes little by little will improve their lives.

There is a quote by Max Lucado. "You change your life by changing your heart." I think it is very important, because it tells you the basic principle that you should fallow to improve yourself. By being better with others it will get you much further than being an asshole. People treat you the way you treat them and you should know that important fact of life. If you do good things, they come back to you. And if you treat others like shit, it comes back to you also. No matter how smart you think you are, no matter how intelligent you think you are. It can always backfire, because the world loves the ones who treat others with respect no matter what their skin color, religion, orientation, flaws, weaknesses or strengths are. You can't just come out to a person and say you are fat. That's rude. You should help someone if he asks you instead. Maybe you know a diet that worked for you, or you know a doctor that helped you to overcome your difficulties. If you can help someone, help someone, but don't criticize them. They know they have a problem, believe me. But calling them fat wouldn't solve their problem; it will only make it worse.

In the real world and in life you can become a good person or a bad one, it's your choice and only you can make it. If you think that a sack of money will solve your problems you are wrong, it could only make them worse. You have to have a plan or an idea, some vision for the future that will empower others and will make the world a better place. No matter what you do, just try to be a better version of yourself tomorrow and you will do great things, meet wonderful people and follow your dreams like never before. Life is hard, but your choices should be easy. Don't put so much pressure on yourself that you can't handle it. Sometimes it's good to break the rules, but you shouldn't hurt anyone by doing that. You might not even know it yet, but someone may be thinking about you right now. Someone might make you the best version of yourself or be with you when the life is tough. After many failures you will understand that nothing in life matters more than people. People are the most valuable gifts in your life and you should do everything to help them, especially if they are close to you. You are a part of the bigger world that depends on you. Maybe on your help, maybe on your good word, maybe on something that is much more important than you think. Everything in this world matters, from the fall of the leaves in the autumn to the first blossom of flowers in spring. None who love nature are bad and no one who has struggles will have those struggles forever. Life is beautiful, just live it.

Some people will tell you that you are worthless, you are good for nothing. But they are wrong. You will be good, you will be strong and you will be caring and nobody will ever doubt your abilities, because you will prove yourself that somehow everything will be good, you will come through, you will prosper and you will make this life better and better for many people. You just have to follow your dreams and reach your goals and start building your ideas for the future.

Maybe you will be someone's back; maybe you will help many people and do something important. You will make mistakes and all of us make them, that's life. Even the best people in the world made mistakes, you are no exception. But every time you fall, you have to stand up, you have to go on. Because only then your life will be complete, you have to have some stance on which you stand for yourself. You have to be great at everything you do. Because only then you will become someone who helps others and someone who inspires others to do great things. You don't have to be the President of America to do big things. You just have to be human. Human in your heart and humane in your work. Sometimes small things matter more than big things. Giving someone hot water if he is cold, making a bed in the morning, preparing lunch for kids, making their lives better day by day. And helping them cope with life's biggest problems will make you become someone who not only can solve your issues, but also help others.

No matter how much you try to overcome your difficulties, they will always be your struggle. You will always have to manage them. No matter what life problems you face. You have to go on and march on. You have to continue.

My name is John and the world that I live in is very different from yours. Now we live in a virtual economy. Or at least 15 percent of the world does. The ones who can afford a virtual life live in a virtual reality called the Virtual Sandbox. People are put into cryogenic states to preserve their bodies and are constantly monitored by nutrition and bowel specialists to keep their vital organs stable. These people choose virtual life, because it gave them the freedom to be anyone they want and live the most luxurious life that anyone can afford. They live in mansions, buy luxury clothes, create virtual brand empires and much more.

The problem is that when the brain is resting, for example like we are sleeping, it enters a certain hibernation mode and turns off. When immersed into the system the brain is constantly in hibernation mode and resting. In the real world the brain faces challenges and neuroplasticity works, but when submerged it loses its ability to send signals through the neurons and the brain functions and abilities decreases to a level of a child and so the brain needs constant challenges to make neuroplasticity work.

And when the brain is immersed in hibernation mode for long periods of time the neurons start to deteriorate and the brain starts to die slowly and the only way to preserve a brain is to live once more in reality, not in the Virtual world.